Stop Monkeying Around

cupcake

For Felix, the best little monkey in the world! - C.S.

For Georgia, Bethany, Emily, Sarah & Abby - S.W.

This edition first published in 2014 by Alligator Books.
Cupcake is an imprint of Alligator Books
Gadd House, Arcadia Avenue, London N3 2JU
www.alligatorbooks.co.uk

Copyright © 2014 Alligator Books

Written by Christine Swift
Illustrated by Sarah Wade

Printed in China 12276

Little monkey was rarely quiet.
He loved to play games, even though the
other animals did not always want to join in.

"Stop monkeying around,"
his mother said! But little monkey was a little monkey!

Little monkey was feeling playful.
He saw elephant drinking at the water hole.

"Stop monkeying around,"

bellowed elephant. "I'm trying to have a drink!"

Snake was trying to curl up for an afternoon nap, but monkey thought it would be fun to swing on his tail.

"Sssssstop monkeying around!"

hissed snake, but little monkey
just laughed and carried on.

Parrot was in the trees, ruffling his beautiful feathers.

Little monkey just couldn't resist trying to pull a feather!

"Stop monkeying around," squawked Parrot. "Leave me alone!"

Tiger was playing with her cubs.
That looks like fun thought monkey.

Monkey swung down and landed on tiger's back, grabbing hold of her tail and pulling at it.

"Stop monkeying around,"

growled tiger, which frightened him a tiny bit.

Monkey felt sad.
Why did nobody want to play?

Hippo was busy
bathing in the mud ...

Giraffe was
busy eating
leaves
from tall
trees...

Even the other monkeys were busy
preening themselves!

Little monkey
asked his mother,
*"What can I do?
Nobody wants to
play with me!"*

"Why don't you make up a game you can play quietly by yourself?" his mother suggested.

"Count some butterflies, swing through the trees!"

So little monkey
sat quietly by
himself.

He counted butterflies...

He counted birds...

He even counted stick insects ...

He swung past the parrot, past the lion,

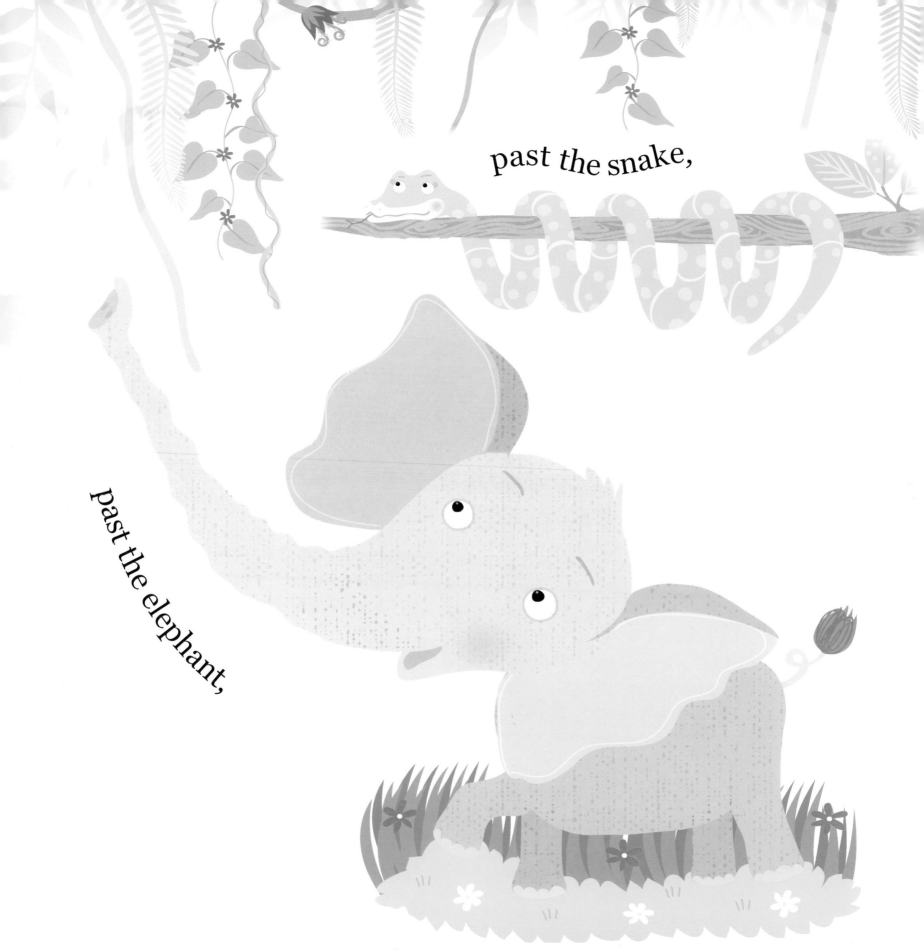

past the snake,

past the elephant,

past the hippo,

past the butterflies,

past the birds,

past the insects,

until...

OOOPS...

he swung smack bang into....

another little monkey, just like him!

Now there were two little monkeys swinging through the trees, but this time they didn't bother anyone else.

They just had great fun playing together!